SAXOPHONE IN E♭ or B♭

TEAM WOODWIND

CORMAC LOANE and RICHARD DUCKETT

IMP

International MUSIC Publications

International Music Publications Limited
Griffin House 161 Hammersmith Road London W6 8BS England

Introduction

The TEAM WOODWIND series has been designed to meet the needs of young wind players everywhere, whether lessons are given individually, in groups or in the classroom.

Musical variety

Each book contains a wide variety of musical styles, from the Baroque and Classical eras to film, folk, jazz and Latin American. In addition there are original pieces and studies, technical exercises and scales, progressing from the beginner stage to approximately Grade IV standard of the *Associated Board of the Royal Schools of Music*. Furthermore TEAM WOODWIND offers material suitable for mixed wind ensemble as well as solos with piano accompaniment.

Ensemble pieces

All TEAM WOODWIND books contain corresponding pages of music which can be played together in harmony. Beginners are thus given early ensemble experience and the opportunity to share lessons with other players, whether they play treble or bass clef, B flat, C or E flat pitched instruments, or even guitar or keyboards.

The ensemble material in the TEAM WOODWIND series integrates with the same material in TEAM BRASS and thus offers exciting possibilities for mixed instrumental lessons, concerts and assemblies.

Duets in TEAM WOODWIND SAXOPHONE are for Eb saxophone. Supplementary parts for B saxophone are located in the Supplement.

Study options

The TEAM WOODWIND series is not a 'method'. It is a selection of primer music from which the teacher can select a suitably graded course for each pupil. This allows for variation in concentration threshold and tempo of progression. There are also several choices of progressive path the pupil can follow. Study options appear at the foot of appropriate pages.

GCSE skills

In addition to fostering musical literacy, Rhythm Grids and Play By Ear lines provide early opportunities for composition and improvisation. This aspect of TEAM WOODWIND can be a useful starting point for these elements in the GCSE examination course now followed in many secondary schools.

Comprehensive notes on the use of this series, scores of ensemble pieces and piano accompaniments are given in the ACCOMPANIMENTS book.

Note:

In some of the earlier pieces in the TEAM WOODWIND solo books the key signatures appear with bracketed sharps or flats. Whereas each key signature is academically correct, the brackets serve to indicate sharps or flats that have not as yet been introduced to the player. These sharps or flats do not appear in the exercise or piece. On the concert pitch cue line of the piano arrangements, however, the key signatures are indicated in the usual way.

Team Woodwind Ensemble

TEAM WOODWIND ensemble material has been specially written so that it can be played by almost any combination of wind instruments that the teacher is likely to encounter. The pieces are basically for duet, to which can be added independent (and inessential) third and fourth parts if required.

The related ensemble parts for the duets in this book will be found in the FLUTE, OBOE and BASSOON books, and in the Supplements to the CLARINET and SAXOPHONE books.

This book also contains ensemble material relating to the duets in TEAM WOODWIND for CLARINET. Relevant parts to the clarinet duets appear on the same numbered pages in all TEAM WOODWIND books, e.g. parts relating to *German tune* (clarinet duet) appear on page 14 in all books. Also, the B flat ensemble material integrates fully with the ensemble material in the TEAM BRASS books. TEAM WOODWIND and TEAM BRASS ensemble can therefore be combined for both small wind/brass groups or for full-sized wind orchestras.

All the ensemble material is graded to match the lesson material. The ensemble pieces may easily be located by following the direction at the foot of the appropriate lesson page. Scores for all ensemble material and more extensive notes appear in the ACCOMPANIMENTS book.

The following symbols have been used to provide an immediate visual identification:

  Pieces with piano accompaniment

  Part of an ensemble arrangement for all C, B flat and E flat instruments (scores included in ACCOMPANIMENTS book)

Because the ensemble pieces provide a meeting point for players who are at various stages of development, these pieces may include technical elements (new notes, rhythms, etc) which are not in fact introduced until some pages later.

Edited by BARRIE CARSON TURNER

Piano accompaniments by GEOFFRY RUSSELL-SMITH and BARRIE CARSON TURNER

INTERNATIONAL MUSIC PUBLICATIONS would like to thank the following publishers for permission to use arrangements
of their copyright material in TEAM WOODWIND.
IN THE MOOD - Words by JOE GARLAND, Music by ANDY RAZAF
© 1939 & 1991 Shapiro Bernstein & Co. Inc., USA
Sub-published by Peter Maurice Music Co. Ltd., London WC2H 0EA
I COULD HAVE DANCED ALL NIGHT - Words by ALAN JAY LERNER, Music by FREDERICK LOEWE
© 1956 & 1991 Alan Jay Lerner and Frederick Loewe
Chappell & Co. Inc., New York, NY, publisher and owner of allied rights throughout the world.
By arrangement with Lowal Corporation. Chappell Music Ltd., London W1Y 3FA
DON'T SIT UNDER THE APPLE TREE (WITH ANYONE ELSE BUT ME) - Words and Music by LEW BROWN, CHARLIE TOBIAS
and SAM H. STEPT
© 1942 & 1991 Robbins Music Corporation USA
Redwood Music Ltd., London NW1 8BD/Memory Lane Music Ltd., London WC2H 8NA/EMI United Partnership Ltd., London WC2H 0EA
STRANGER ON THE SHORE - Words by ROBERT MELLIN, Music by ACKER BILK
© 1962 & 1991 EMI Music Publishing Ltd, London WC2H 0EA
MOONLIGHT SERENADE - Words by MITCHELL PARISH, Music by GLENN MILLER
© 1939 & 1991 Robbins Music Corporation, USA
EMI United Partnership Ltd., London WC2H 0EA
MOOD INDIGO - Words and Music by DUKE ELLINGTON, IRVING MILLS and ALBANY BIGARD
© 1931 & 1991 Gotham Music Service Inc, USA
Sub-published by EMI Music Publishing Ltd., London WC2H 0EA
WHAT A WONDERFUL WORLD - Words and Music by GEORGE DAVID WEISS & BOB THIELE
© 1967 & 1991 Herald Square Music Company, USA
Carlin Music Corp., London NW1 8BD
WATERMELON MAN - Music by HERBIE HANCOCK, Words by JIMI HENDRIX
© 1962 & 1991 Hancock Music Co.
B. Feldman & Co. Ltd., London WC2H 0EA
BLOWIN' IN THE WIND - Words and Music by BOB DYLAN
© 1963 & 1991 Witmark & Sons, USA
Warner Chappell Music Ltd., London W1Y 3FA
EDELWEISS (From THE SOUND OF MUSIC) - Lyrics by OSCAR HAMMERSTEIN II, Music by RICHARD RODGERS
Copyright © 1959 by Richard Rodgers and Oscar Hammerstein II
Copyright Renewed.
This arrangement Copyright © 1991 by WILLIAMSON MUSIC CO.
WILLIAMSON MUSIC owner of publication and allied rights throughout the world.
International Copyright Secured   All Rights Reserved
LOVE ME TENDER - Words and Music by VERA MATSON & ELVIS PRESLEY
© 1956 & 1991 Elvis Presley Music Inc., USA
Carlin Music Corp., London NW1 8BD
LITTLE DONKEY - Words and Music by ERIC BOSWELL
© 1959 & 1991 Chappell Music Ltd., London W1Y 3FA
THE PINK PANTHER - by HENRY MANCINI
© 1963 & 1991 United Artists Music Co. Inc., USA
EMI United Partnership Ltd., London WC2H 0EA
OVER THE RAINBOW - Words by E. Y. HARBURG, Music by HAROLD ARLEN
© 1938 & 1991 Leo Feist Inc., USA
EMI United Partnership Ltd., London WC2H 0EA
SWEET GEORGIA BROWN - Words and Music by BEN BERNIE, KENNETH CASEY & MACEO PINKARD
© 1925 & 1991 Remick Music Corp, USA
Sub-published by Francis Day & Hunter Ltd., London WC2H 0EA and Redwood Music Ltd., London NW1 8BD
STAR WARS Main Title - by JOHN WILLIAMS
© 1977 & 1991 Fox Fanfare Music Inc.
Warner Chappell Music Ltd., London W1Y 3FA

Sincere thanks are extended to the following people whose criticism, advice and help in various ways has been invaluable.
KEITH ALLEN, Head of Music Services for the City of Birmingham Education Department.
PHILIP BROOKES, Bassoonist.
PETER BULLOCK, Clarinet Teacher, Derbyshire County Education Department.
RICHARD REAKES, Oboe Teacher, City of Birmingham Education Department.
DAVID ROBINSON, Woodwind Teacher, Kirklees Education Department.
JULIE SCHRODER, Flute Teacher, City of Birmingham Education Department.
ALISON WHATLEY, Oboe Teacher, City of Birmingham Education Department.
And also to the many pupils who have worked with the TEAM WOODWIND books in transcript form.

First Published 1991

© International Music Publications Limited,
Griffin House, 161 Hammersmith Road, London W6 8BS, England.

Cover Design: Ian Barrett / David Croft
Cover Photography: Ron Goldby
Production: Stephen Clark / David Croft
Reprographics: Cloverleaf
Instruments photographed by courtesy of Vincent Bach International Ltd., London.
Typeset by Cromwell Typesetting & Design Ltd., London / Printed in England by Halstan & Co. Ltd.

TEAM WOODWIND: Saxophone in Eb or Bb
ISBN 1-84328-640-8 / Order Ref: 17535/215-2-656

Getting started

What to do with the reed and the mouthpiece

Wet the reed by putting it in your mouth. Place the ligature onto the mouthpiece. Tighten the screws so that the reed is kept firmly in place on the mouthpiece.

How to put the Saxophone together

1. Put the mouthpiece onto the crook using a gentle, twisting motion.

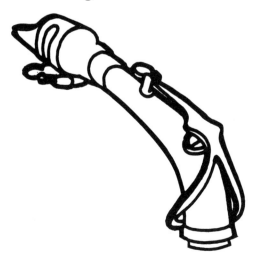

2. Carefully twist the crook
   onto the main body of
   the saxophone.

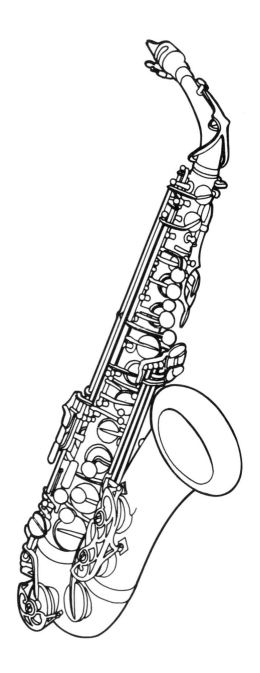

Look in a mirror to check
that you are holding the
saxophone the way your
teacher tells you.

Listening skills

There's no better way to start a music lesson than to play some listening games. They help you to listen very carefully and are a good starting point for improvisation, in jazz or other styles. You can play the games with your teacher or/and with other pupils, in large or small groups. You won't use written music of course, but the printed examples below might help to show you how to get started.

I got rhythm

The first player plays a short rhythm on one note and the second player (or group) repeats it. If you play in a group, each player in turn can make up a new rhythm while the others listen and repeat it.

Question and answer

The first player plays a short rhythm on one note and the second player answers with a different rhythm. In a group lesson, simply play in turn.

Action replay

The first player plays a short tune on, say, three notes and the second player or group repeats it. In a group, each player in turn can make up a new tune while the others listen and repeat it.

Hands off

The first player makes up a short tune using three or four notes and the next player has to answer it with a different tune. In a group, each player in turn can make up a new tune.

Start with B . . .

Clap, say,*
and play
the rhythm

* French time names may be used

The TIME SIGNATURE 4/4 means each bar must add up to FOUR beats

A CROTCHET (or QUARTER-NOTE) lasts for ONE beat

A MINIM (or HALF-NOTE) lasts for TWO beats

A CROTCHET REST lasts for ONE beat

A COMMA means take a breath

bar 1 bar 2 bar 3 bar 4

PULSE-clap or beat time

. . . then on to A

The note G

G, A and B March

A SEMIBREVE (or WHOLE-NOTE) lasts for FOUR beats

Merrily we roll along

Traditional

Au clair de la lune

Traditional

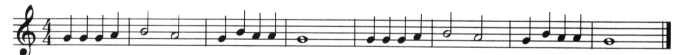

Tricky tune

■ Proceed to F on page 6; or C on page 5.

The note C

Go and tell aunt Rhody

Traditional

Flowing

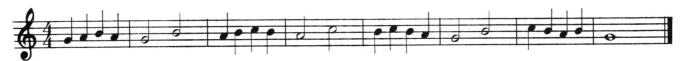

Walking

Sort 'em out!

March tempo

■ Proceed to D on page 7; or B♭ on page 16.

The note F

Merrily we roll along

Traditional

Acapulco Bay

Acapulco Bay can be played in conjunction with the same piece on page 16.

The note D

Press octave
key

Welsh tune

Traditional

Step round

(1) (2) (3) (4)

'C' means Common Time i.e. 4/4 time

play by ear

The two dots mean that the music should be repeated

Jazzily

Continue

Brightly

Continue

Upper E

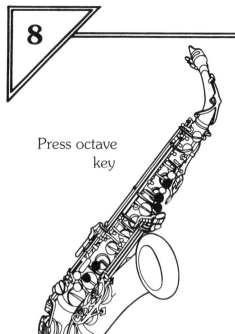

Press octave key

Pattern

| Phrase A | Phrase B | Phrase A repeated | Phrase C |

Slow round

(1) (2)

Slowly ... Continue

Merrily ... Continue

■ Quavers on page 18; Ensemble material up to E on page 20; Slurs on page 13.

The note F#

The SHARP raises the pitch of a note by one semitone

The key signature of G major

Sharks!

The sharp affects all F's up to the bar line

The sharp on the top line makes all the F's sharp

One man and his dog

Traditional

Jazz/blues improvisation (1)

When you improvise music you make it up yourself as you go along. You might already have done some of this while playing the Listening Games, and in fact that is exactly how we start to improvise in a Blues or Jazz style – by copying or answering another player's phrases. In this way we can gradually build up a large catalogue of jazzy phrases for future use.

The easiest way to start improvising is to play in jazz style the four exercises that appeared on the Listening Games pages – *I got rhythm*, *Question and answer*, *Action replay* and *Hands off*. To do this you need to put your quavers into 'swing' style, so 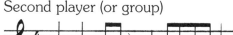 becomes  (which is called a triplet). Swing style quavers are *written* in the normal way as 'straight' quavers; but you play them differently. Your teacher will demonstrate the following phrases in 'swing' style:

I got rhythm

First player

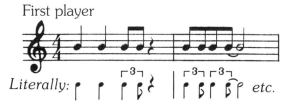

Second player (or group)

Question and answer

First player

Second player

Action replay

First player

Second player (or group)

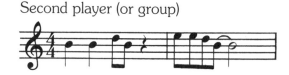

Hands off

First player

Second player

If you now play some of your phrases with an accompaniment on piano or keyboard, in twelve bar blues style (in D) you will hear that your note G seems to fit and not to fit at the same time! This is because the note A in HANDS OFF is known as a blue note – that is to say, it sound a little 'off-key'. These are the chords that your keyboard player will need to use:

(Use 'swing' setting on keyboard)

D7	D7	D7	D7	G7	G7	D7	D7	A7	G7	D7	D7

(Alternatively, use D minor & G minor)

If there is no piano or keyboard in your practice room then ask someone to record the accompaniment for you.

If you learn in a group, let each player play a two bar phrase in turn. Or your teacher might play two bars and the group reply, and so on. The important thing is to *listen to one another* and *keep in time*.

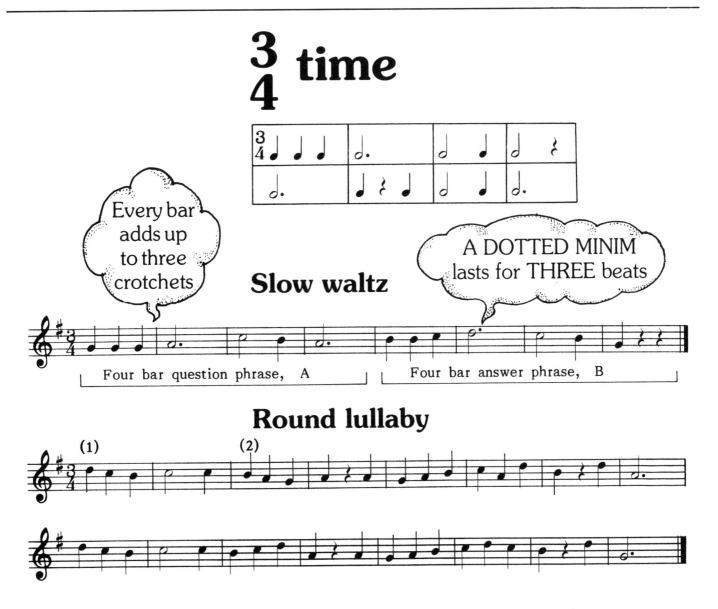

Every bar adds up to three crotchets

A DOTTED MINIM lasts for THREE beats

Slow waltz

Four bar question phrase, A   Four bar answer phrase, B

Round lullaby

(1)   (2)

■ For related ensemble material see page 14; Quavers on page 18.

Low E

Yo heave ho!

Traditional

This means 'rest' for 4 whole bars – so count ① 2 3 ② 2 3 ③ 2 3 ④ 2 3 and then play from bar 5

Les ballons

Gently and dreamily

Getting slower

■ Low D on page 22.

Slurs

The notes covered by a SLUR are played smoothly and in one breath, with only the first note being tongued

Slur round

Morning

EDVARD GRIEG (1843-1907)

Victorian ballad

German tune
Duet

Traditional

Lullaby
Duet

■ Tunes carrying the symbol ⊕ can be played with the same named tunes in the other TEAM WOODWIND and TEAM BRASS books. 3rd parts for B♭ TENOR SAXOPHONE can be found in the SAXOPHONE SUPPLEMENT.

Tied notes

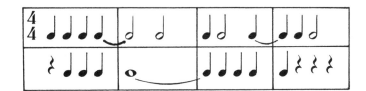

A minim tied to a crotchet lasts for 3 beats

A crotchet tied to a crotchet lasts for 2 beats

A semibreve tied to a crotchet lasts for 5 beats and so on

Don't be late!

Canzonetta

Duet

Compose a part for tambour or tambourine

Fast
(Polyphonic texture)

soft

COUNT
① 2 3 4   ② 2 3 4

soft

A (Homophonic texture)

loud

loud

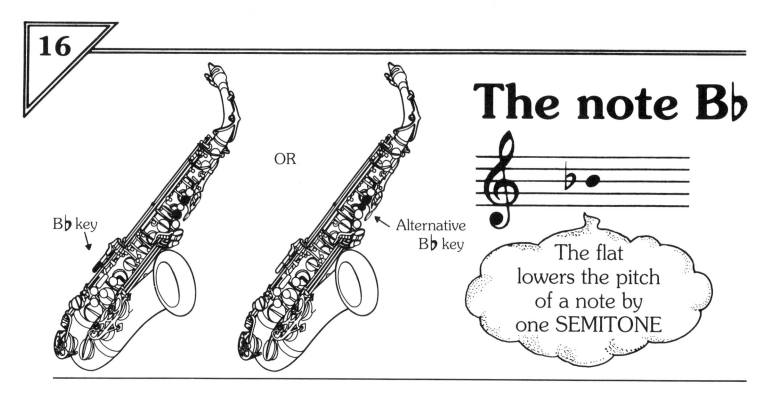

The note B♭

The flat lowers the pitch of a note by one SEMITONE

Acapulco Bay

This piece can be played in conjunction with *Acapulco Bay* on page 6.

Tempo de beguine

fairly loud

Ode to joy

LUDWIG VAN BEETHOVEN
(1770-1827)

fairly soft

In the key of F major all the B's are flat

Twinkle, twinkle, little star

Traditional

Round

fairly loud

Upper F

Press octave key

Scale and arpeggio of F major

Lasst uns erfreuen

Traditional

■ Proceed to F♯ on page 23; or G on pages 23 & 24.

Quavers

Skip to my Lou

Traditional

Sleigh ride

Related ensemble material on page 20; Quavers in $\frac{6}{8}$ on page 36.

Jazz/blues improvisation (2)

Jazz musicians always do a lot of practice on their own, often without any kind of accompaniment. You should do this too, although you might find it easier to play along with a pre-recorded accompaniment, if this can be arranged.

In performance, jazz is normally played by a group of musicians. There is usually a 'theme' (a tune which keeps coming back) which everyone plays once or twice to start with and perhaps again at the end. The improvisation takes place in the middle, with each player performing in turn. A plan of the performance might look like this:

THEME	IMPROVISATION	THEME
(played once or twice)	(each player in turn)	(or variation on theme)

Here is a twelve bar blues theme. Play it with other musicians.

After you have played the theme through a couple of times try improvising in the way described on page 10. By now you are probably ready to use more notes, so here is part of the jazz scale of E (G at concert pitch). Try to memorise it. First practise it by simply playing up and down the scale several times using various repeated jazz rhythms:

Here are some examples of jazz phrases you might play using these notes. Your teacher will play them for you first.

You can change the rhythms in these phrases to make them different, or perhaps play the same rhythm and change the notes. Of course you can also improvise your own new phrases.

This is the accompaniment you can use which will fit both the theme and your improvisation:

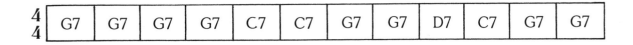

$\frac{4}{4}$	G7	G7	G7	G7	C7	C7	G7	G7	D7	C7	G7	G7

Regal fanfare

*Fanfare part for timpani (or bass drum and tenor drum) and cymbals.

¢ means TWO MINIM BEATS in each bar, i.e. $\frac{2}{2}$ time, (sometimes called ALLA BREVE time)

When I first came to this land

Duet

Traditional

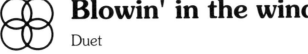

On the repeat, omit these bars and go straight to the bar marked 2

Blowin' in the wind

Duet

Words and Music
by BOB DYLAN

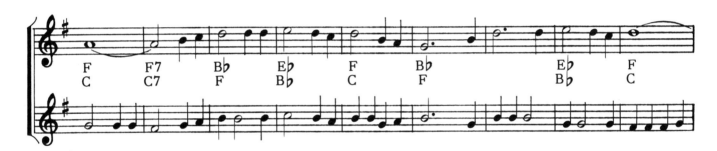

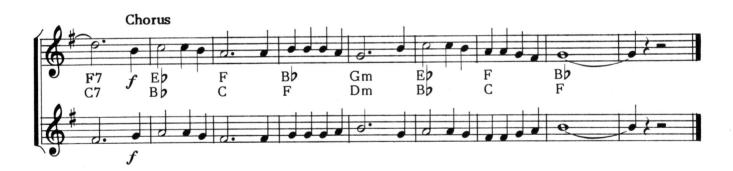

Play by ear

Low D

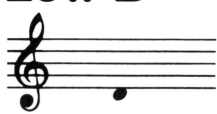

Amazing grace

Traditional

Slowly

Eb accompt. Bb   Bb7   Eb   Bb   F   F7
Bb accompt.   F   F7   Bb   F   C   C7

Bb   Bb7   Eb   Bb   F7   Bb
F   F7   Bb   F   C7   F

The QUAVER TRIPLET means that three quavers are played in the time of one crotchet

Polovtsian dance

ALEXANDER BORODIN
(1833-1887)

Lilting, not fast

mp (mf)

Press octave key

Upper F♯

Press octave key

Upper G

Scale and arpeggio of G major

Barcarolle

JACQUES OFFENBACH
(1819-1880)

Flowing

Related ensemble material on page 37.

Sing hosanna

Traditional

Edelweiss

from *The Sound of Music*

Lyrics by OSCAR HAMMERSTEIN II
Music by RICHARD RODGERS

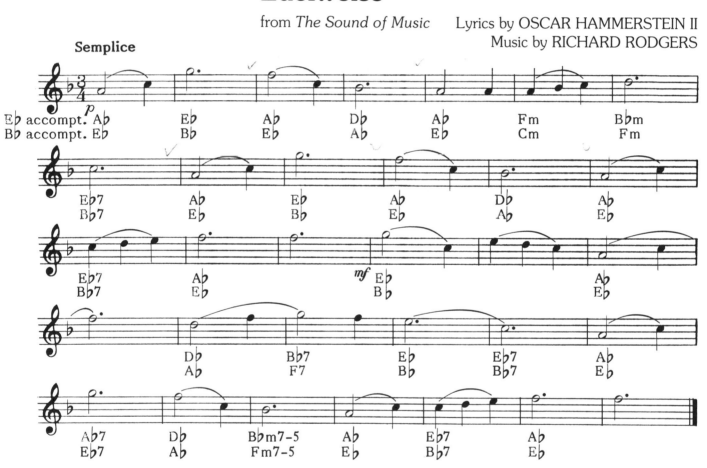

Upper A

Press octave key

Wiegenlied

Traditional

Happily

slowing down   back to first speed

Frère Jacques

Traditional

Brightly

Away in a manger

WILLIAM JAMES KIRKPATRICK
(1838-1921)

Semplice

Dotted crotchets

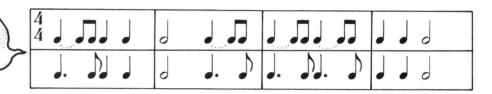

Make up your own melodies using dotted rhythms

New World Symphony

ANTONIN DVOŘÁK
(1841-1904)

Join the dots to make the dotted-crotchet/ quaver effect

Deck the halls

Traditional

Auld lang syne

Traditional

Play by ear

Related ensemble material on pages 48 & 49; dotted quavers on page 34.

Jazz/blues improvisation (3)

Miles ahead

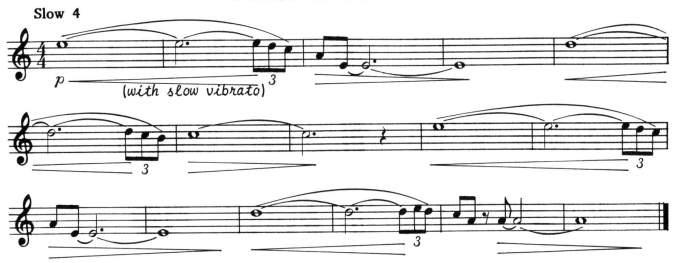

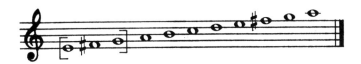

You can improvise using the notes from this jazz scale which was popularised by the jazz musician Miles Davis. Some suggestions, using scales and arpeggios are given below.

This piano/keyboard accompaniment can be used for *Miles ahead* and for improvisation with E♭ saxophone.

Low C

Low C key

The old hundredth

Traditional

Unto us a boy is born

Traditional

Canon

THOMAS TALLIS (c. 1505-1585)

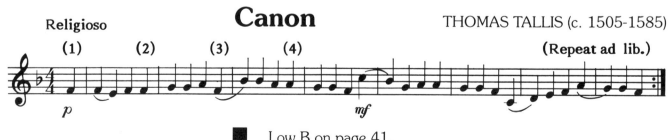

Low B on page 41.

The note C♯

The key signature of D major

No keys are pressed down for this note

Scale and arpeggio of D major

Love me tender

Words and Music by
VERA MATSON & ELVIS PRESLEY

| E♭ accompt. | F | | G7 | C7 | F | F |
| B♭ accompt. | C | | D7 | G7 | C | C |

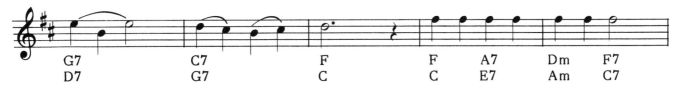

| G7 | | C7 | | F | F | A7 | Dm | F7 |
| D7 | | G7 | | C | C | E7 | Am | C7 |

| B♭ | | A7 | D7 | Gm | C7 | F |
| F | | E7 | A7 | Dm | G7 | C |

Coventry carol

Traditional

Moderato

Good King Wenceslas

Traditional

Over the rainbow

Words by E. Y. HARBURG
Music by HAROLD ARLEN

Jazz/blues improvisation (4)

This new blues scale is in the key of G.

The additional note A may be used if you wish. Once again, start by playing the scale up and down using a variety of jazz rhythms. Then start to improvise some two/four bar phrases, perhaps using the 'question and answer' method:

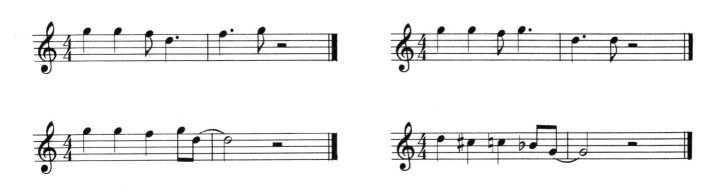

Once you have built up a number of improvised phrases try them out within the piece below. It is called *He's a city slicker*.

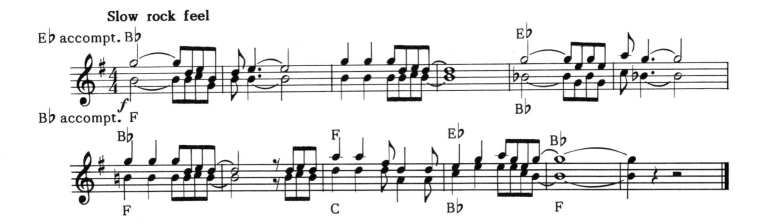

Semiquavers in 2/4

Semiquavers are sometimes
called SIXTEENTH-NOTES

Semiquaver study

> Join the dots in order to make 'ties' as and when required

Related ensemble material on pages 48 & 55.

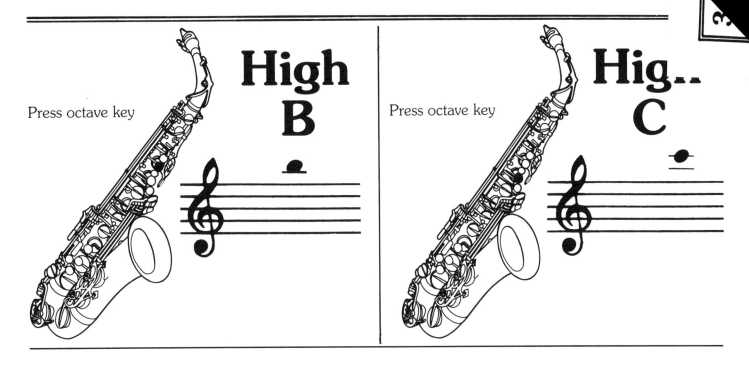

Press octave key

High B

Press octave key

High C

Scale and arpeggio of C major

The first Nowell

Traditional

Brightly

Yankee Doodle

Traditional

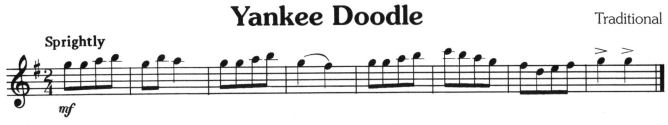

Sprightly

■ Proceed to High C♯ and High D on page 46; related ensemble material on pages 48 & 49 or dotted quavers on page 34; or $\frac{6}{8}$ on page 36.

The dotted quaver

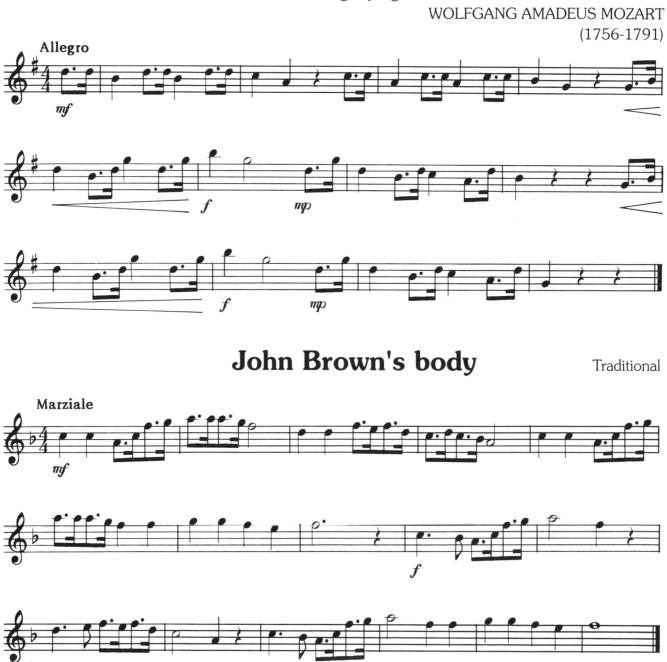

Say 'goodbye'

from *The Marriage of Figaro*

WOLFGANG AMADEUS MOZART
(1756-1791)

Allegro

John Brown's body

Traditional

Marziale

■ Related ensemble material on page 55.

The notes E♭ & Upper E♭

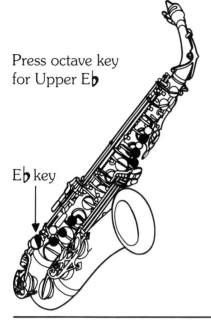

Press octave key
for Upper E♭

E♭ key

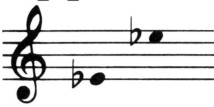

The key signature of E♭ major

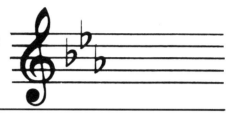

$\frac{6}{8}$ Time

and its relationship with $\frac{2}{4}$ time

$\frac{2}{4}$ means that every bar adds up to TWO CROTCHET BEATS

In $\frac{2}{4}$ time quavers are grouped in twos, to make up ONE CROTCHET BEAT

$\frac{6}{8}$ time means every bar adds up to TWO DOTTED CROTCHET BEATS

In $\frac{6}{8}$ time quavers are grouped in THREES to make up ONE DOTTED CROTCHET BEAT

When Johnny comes marching home

Traditional

Lively

Play by ear

Moderately

Related ensemble material on page 39; more $\frac{6}{8}$ on page 43.

Au clair de la lune

Traditional

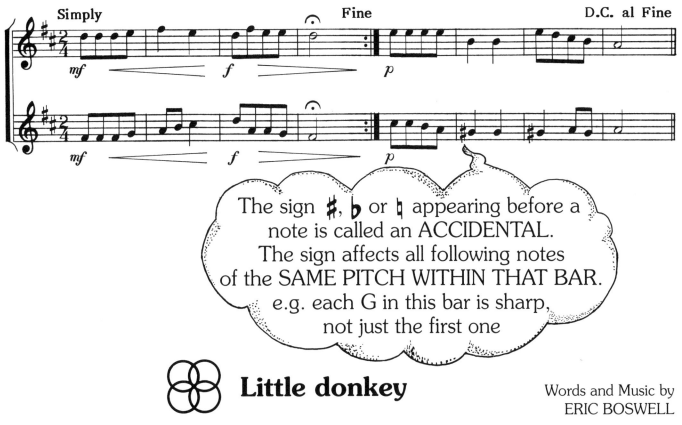

Little donkey

Words and Music by
ERIC BOSWELL

The sign ♯, ♭ or ♮ appearing before a note is called an ACCIDENTAL. The sign affects all following notes of the SAME PITCH WITHIN THAT BAR. e.g. each G in this bar is sharp, not just the first one

Quaver syncopation

To be played:
(a) In strict time
(b) In swing time

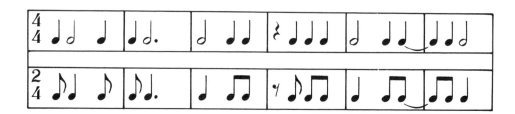

Old Liza Jane

Bright and rhythmic

Caribbean dance

Traditional

Tempo di Rumba

Fine

D.C. al Fine

Syncopated crotchets on pages 15 & 21; related ensemble material on page 39.

Tijuana brass

I saw three ships

Traditional

The notes G♯ & Upper G♯

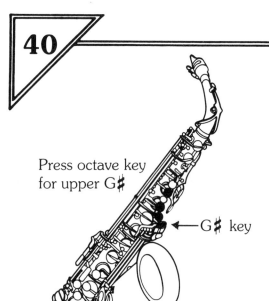

Press octave key for upper G♯

← G♯ key

Allegretto

ANTONIO DIABELLI (1781-1858)

The key signature of A major

Rigaudon

HENRY PURCELL (1659-1695)

Simply blue

Twelve bar blues

Accompaniment for keyboard on 'Jazz Rock' setting

Bars						
3	5	2	2	1	1	1
Fm	Fm	B♭m	Fm	C7	B♭m	Fm

Chords

D blues scale for improvisation

Low B

Low C key

Low B key

God save the Queen

Traditional

Slowly

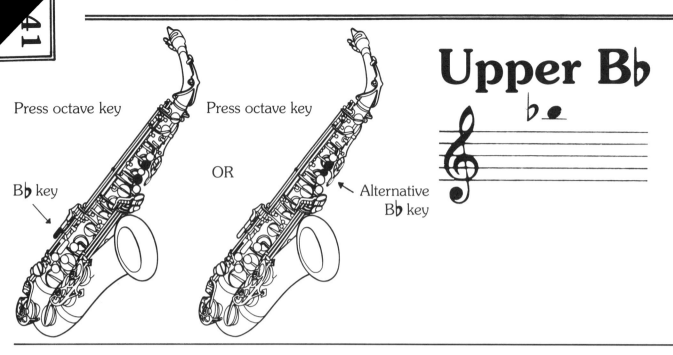

Upper B♭

Press octave key

Press octave key

OR

B♭ key

Alternative B♭ key

Scale and arpeggio of B♭ major

The key signature of B♭ major

Joy to the world

GEORGE FRIDERIC HANDEL
(1685-1759)

Joyfully

Canon

GUSTAV MAHLER
(1860-1911)

Langsam
(1)

(2)

Low B♭

Low C key

Low B♭ key

Scale and arpeggio of B♭ major

Three blind mice

Traditional

Low C#

One man and another dog!

Brightly

mf

What a wonderful world

Words and Music by
GEORGE DAVID WEISS
& BOB THIELE

Relaxed, easy tempo

mf

| Eb accompt. | F | | Bb | Csus | C7 | F | Am | Bb | F | Gm | C7 | F | A7 | Dm | Db |
| Bb accompt. | C | | F | Gsus | G7 | C | Em | F | C | Dm | G7 | C | E7 | Am | Ab |

To Coda

| G7sus | C7 | | F | G7 | | C7 | | F | Am | Bb | F | Gm | C7 | F | A7 | Dm |
| D7sus | G7 | | C | D7 | | G7 | | C | Em | F | C | Dm | G7 | C | E7 | Am |

| Db | | | F/C | C7 | | F | | | | C | | | F | |
| Ab | | | C/G | G7 | | C | | | | G | | | C | |

cresc. *dim.* D.S. al Coda *rit.*

| C | | | F | *f* | Dm | Am | Dm | Am | E7 | Am | Bbm | C7 |
| G | | | C | | Am | Em | Am | Em | B7 | Em | Fm | G7 |

CODA *rit.*

| F | A7 | Dm | | F7-5 | Bbmaj7 | G7 | | C7sus | C7 | | F | F7 | Bb | F |
| C | E7 | Am | | C7-5 | Fmaj7 | D7 | | G7sus | G7 | | C | C7 | F | C |

Two Bizet themes

from *L'Arlésienne suite No. 1*

GEORGES BIZET
(1838-1875)

Allegro deciso

Andante molto

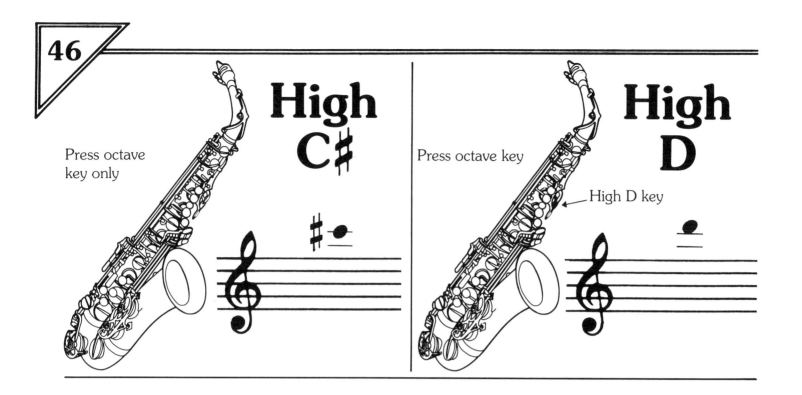

High C#

Press octave key only

High D

Press octave key

High D key

Star Wars main title

by JOHN WILLIAMS

$\frac{5}{4}$ time

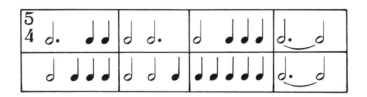

Waiting!

Scarboro' five

Repeat or improvise ad lib.

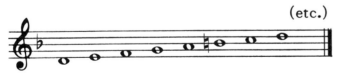

(etc.)

You can improvise using the notes of this D Dorian Scale with a variety of jazz rhythms and long notes. The piano/keyboard accompaniment below can be used for *Scarboro' five* and for improvisation, with E♭ saxophone.

Very rhythmic

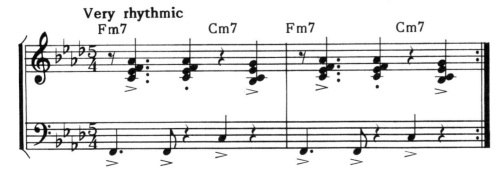

Repeat/improvise ad libitum

Michael row the boat ashore

Traditional

Canzona

ADRIANO BANCHIERI (1568-1634)

Part 1

Canzona

Part 2

Compose an accompaniment for Tambour using crotchets, quavers and semiquavers

■ Because the *Canzona* is a four-part polyphonic piece, the parts above cannot be played simply as a saxophone duet. Third and fourth parts are to be found, however, in the SAXOPHONE SUPPLEMENT and BASSOON book.

O little town of Bethlehem

Traditional

 ## St. Anthony chorale

JOSEPH HAYDN
(1732-1809)

Scale and arpeggio of F major (12th)

West Indian carnival

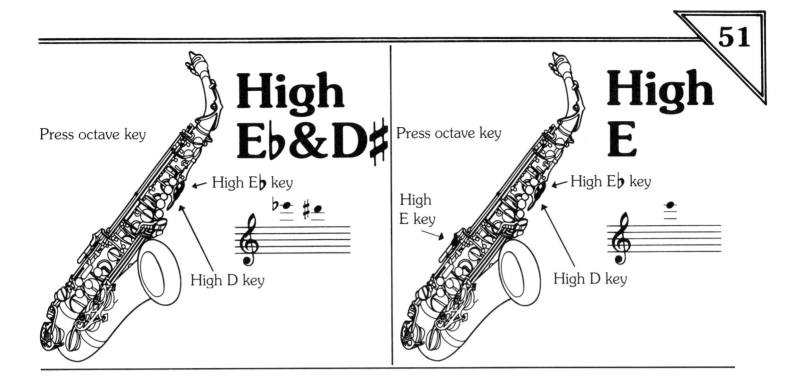

The swinger

Accompaniment for keyboard on '16' beat rhythm setting

$\frac{4}{4}$

Bars					
4	2	2	1	1	2
Abm	Dbm	Abm	Eb-13	Dbm	Abm

Chords

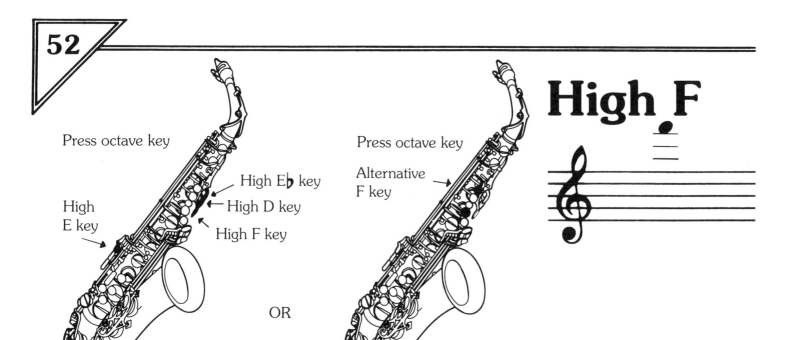

High F

Press octave key

High E♭ key

High D key

High F key

High E key

OR

Press octave key

Alternative F key

Romance

WOLFGANG AMADEUS MOZART
(1756-1791)

Andante

Chromatics
Chromatic scale of D

Play the scale using different rhythms.

Blue monk

THELONIUS MONK
(1920-1982)

After you have played through the tune, improvise on the same chord sequence, using the G blues scale (given on page 31). Then play the tune again to finish.

Moonlight serenade

Words by MITCHELL PARISH
Music by GLENN MILLER

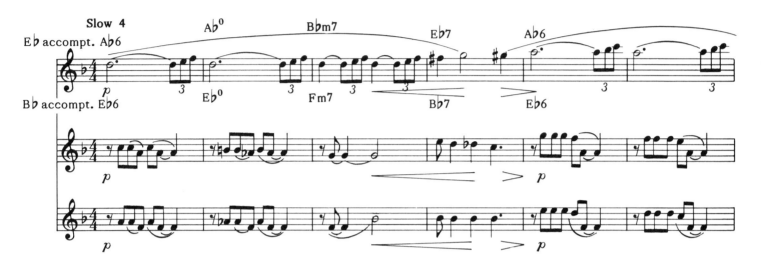

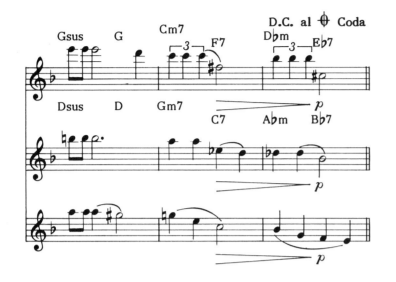

March

from *Judas Maccabaeus*

GEORGE FRIDERIC HANDEL
(1685-1759)

Bolero

MAURICE RAVEL (1875-1937)

Tempo di bolero, moderato assai

Pomp and Circumstance March No. 1

EDWARD ELGAR (1857-1934)

Scales and arpeggios

Scale and arpeggio of C major

Scale and arpeggio of G major

Scale and arpeggio of D major

Scale of A minor harmonic

Arpeggio of A minor

Scale of E minor harmonic

Arpeggio of E minor

Scale of D minor harmonic

Arpeggio of D minor

Scale of C minor harmonic

Arpeggio of C minor

The Pink Panther

by HENRY MANCINI

In the mood

Words by JOE GARLAND
Music by ANDY RAZAF

Take turns at playing 8 bar solos over these chords using notes of the blues scale below.

Then D.𝄋. al ⊕ Coda

Repeat several times from 𝄋 reducing the dynamic each time. The last time play *ff*.

F Blues scale

Watermelon man

HERBIE HANCOCK

After you have played through the tune, take turns at improvising while the chord sequence is played on the keyboard. Improvise using notes from the D blues scale:

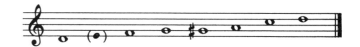

SUPPLEMENT

International MUSIC Publications

International Music Publications Limited
Griffin House 161 Hammersmith Road London W6 8BS England

German tune

Traditional

3rd B♭ part with B♭/E♭ duet

Notes with Stems up: 3rd part;
Stems down: 4th part; Two Stems: Both parts in Unison.

3rd & 4th E♭ part with B♭/E♭ duet

3rd part

4th part

Lullaby

3rd B♭ part with B♭/E♭ duet

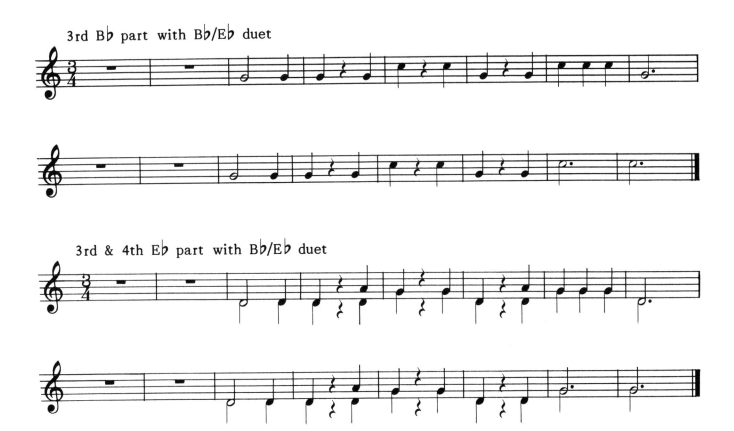

3rd & 4th E♭ part with B♭/E♭ duet

Canzonetta

3rd B♭ part with B♭/E♭ duet

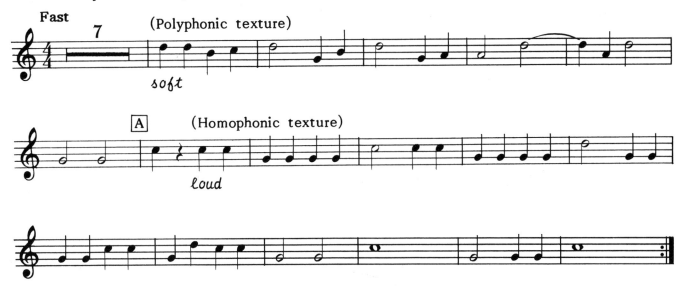

15

Canzonetta

3rd E♭ part with B♭/E♭ duet

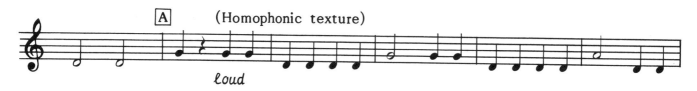

20

Regal fanfare

4th B♭ part with B♭/E♭ trio

3rd. E♭ part with B♭/E♭ trio

When I first came to this land

Traditional

3rd B♭ part with B♭/E♭ duet

Fast and furious

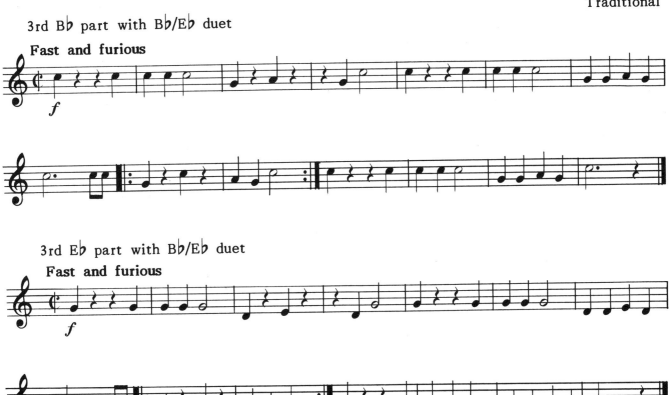

3rd E♭ part with B♭/E♭ duet

Fast and furious

 # Blowin' in the wind

Words and music by
BOB DYLAN

3rd B♭ part with B♭/E♭ duet

Steadily

Chorus

Blowin' in the wind

3rd & 4th E♭ part with B♭/E♭ duet

Steadily

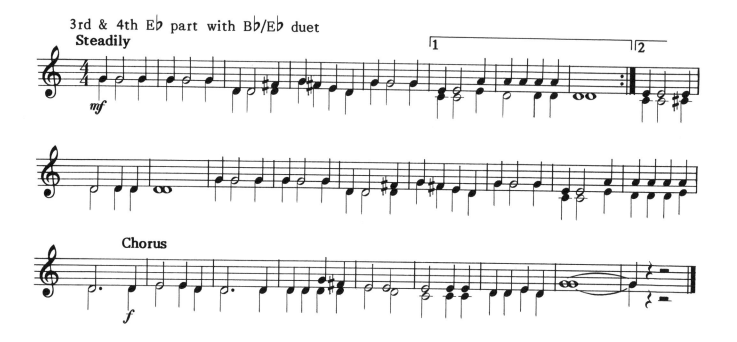

Chorus

Au clair de la lune

3rd B♭ part with B♭/E♭ duet

Traditional

Simply ... Fine ... D.C. al Fine

3rd & 4th E♭ part with B♭/E♭ duet

Simply ... Fine ... D.C. al Fine

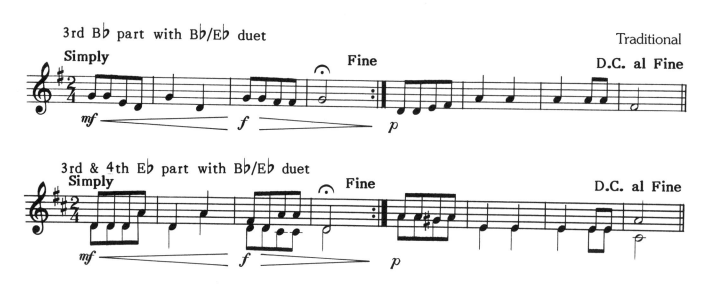

Little donkey

Words and music by
ERIC BOSWELL

3rd B♭ part with B♭/E♭ duet

3rd & 4th E♭ part with B♭/E♭ duet

Tijuana brass

3rd B♭ part with B♭/E♭ duet

Tijuana brass

3rd & 4th E♭ part with B♭/E♭ duet

Brightly

D.C. al Fine

I saw three ships

Traditional

3rd B♭ part with B♭/E♭ duet

Happily

3rd E♭ part with B♭/E♭ duet

Happily

Michael row the boat ashore

Traditional

3rd B♭ part with B♭/E♭ duet

Moderately

3rd & 4th E♭ part with B♭/E♭ duet

Moderately

Canzona

ADRIANO BANCHIERI
(1568–1634)

4th B♭ part with B♭/E♭ duet

3rd E♭ part with B♭/E♭ duet

O little town of Bethlehem

3rd B♭ part with B♭/E♭ duet

Traditional

3rd E♭ part with B♭/E♭ duet

St. Anthony Chorale

JOSEPH HAYDN
(1732–1809)

3rd B♭ part with B♭/E♭ duet

3rd & 4th E♭ part with B♭/E♭ duet

March from *Judas Maccabaeus*

GEORGE FRIDERIC HANDEL
(1685–1759)